MONDAY SURVIVAL GUIDE

J.H. GLAZE

ISBN: 978-0-9974105-0-1

Cover Concept and Design: J.H. Glaze
Scratchboard Art: Dave Felton
Editor: Susan Grimm

First Printing March 2016
Published by MostCool Media Inc.
Make it interesting. Make it MostCool.

Proudly printed in the United States of America.

First Edition March 2016

10 9 8 7 6 5 4 3 2 1

Thank You!

Thank you reader, for your support. I appreciate each of you and always enjoy hearing your thoughts, so don't hesitate to voice your opinions.

Many thanks to a few coworkers who inspired some of the main characters in this story, Drew Anthony, Angela Christman-Wilson, and Greg Petrirena. These are some of the people who encourage me and push me to be a better person.

I hope I portrayed them as they would like, but of course even though I used their names, the characters are entirely fictional.

As always, thank you Susan, the best editor on the whole damn planet, and my best friend.

If you enjoy this story, you may want to try the full-length novels, novellas and short stories by J.H. Glaze. Available on Amazon.com & other online retailers in eBook and Paperback.

Visit the pages of J.H. Glaze:

www.JHGlaze.com

Facebook: Author J.H. Glaze

Follow on Twitter: @themostcoolone

Search for JH Glaze on Google for more!

Thanks For Reading! Reviews on Amazon and other sites are greatly appreciated. Please tell your friends about Author J.H. Glaze books.

MONDAY SURVIVAL GUIDE

J.H. GLAZE

ONE

About thirty minutes into the workday, the entire floor of the building was suddenly awash with a flash of intense light from outside.

"What the hell was that?" Rick lifted his hand to his eyes, but by then, the light was gone.

"It was like a flash from some giant camera, but there's nothing out there," Al replied from the cubicle behind him.

Rick turned around to see the man standing at the window and rose to look for himself. Scanning the landscape outside, he sensed that others around him were headed for the windows too. A few rows away, someone commented, "That's weird."

All at once, the floor became silent except for the overhead lights, which made a clicking sound as they went dark.

"Must have been a transformer blowing out somewhere. That could make the power go off," Al offered, trying to make sense of it.

Someone else across the room was explaining his theory. "Probably total overload of the power grid. They've been predicting something like this would happen for years."

There was no comment from his co-workers so he said it again, only louder. "It must be the grid. There isn't any sign of wind out there, some clouds, but no rain. I think we can rule out lightning on this one."

Rick pulled his phone from his pocket to see what time it was, but when he pressed the button, nothing happened.

"Damn, I forgot to charge my phone again. Marie, do you have the time?" He pointed at his wrist and then at hers.

Looking at her watch as requested, she tapped at the crystal. "It isn't working. I think the battery is dead."

"Was it dead when you put it on this morning?"

"I don't remember."

"What time does it say?"

"8:35. Wait. That's just about right, isn't it?"

Rick felt his pulse quicken, his heart thumping hard in his chest. If his suspicion was correct, it was going to be a very bad

Monday. He decided to go find to his brother. Instinctively, he headed for the elevators and pushed the button. Ray worked on the tenth floor. Without thinking, he pushed the button again when it didn't light up the first time.

"Shit, what am I thinking? The power's off."

Checking around for the stairs, which he never used except for fire drills, he spotted the red exit sign and hurried down the hall toward the stairwell door.

"Rick, how long do you think the power's going to be off?" Angela trotted up from behind him and positioned herself between him and the door. "I'm supposed to be on a conference call with the Chicago office at nine. I don't want Sherena up my ass about being late to the call again."

"Listen, Angie. If I'm right, you are going to have much more to worry about than Sherena."

"What are you talking about? Is this one of those apocalypse things you and your brother have been yapping about for the last couple of years? If it is…"

"I… I don't know yet. I'm about to go get Ray. After that, I need to go outside to check on something before I know more. I wouldn't want to freak you out."

He opened the door to the stairway and stepped through, leaving her there to talk to herself. Just as he started up the steps, he heard the door below open again.

"Rick, wait up! If there's some shit going down, I don't want to be left trying to get home by myself." She was puffing as she caught up to him. "What do you think this is?"

"So far, I am guessing an EMP, but I won't know for sure until I get to the parking deck."

She stepped in sync with him, but stumbled as she tried to look him in the eye.

"Hey man, I know we use acronyms out the ass around here, but if this is the end of the world, I would like to know what the fuck is an EMP!"

He stopped on the last set of steps before the door to the tenth floor. "Look, I'm going to explain it to you quick because every second counts if this is true. An EMP is an Electromagnetic Pulse. It can happen from extreme solar flares, or from a nuke exploding a mile or so above the earth. That would explain the flash."

"A nuke? Shouldn't we be looking for a shelter?"

"No, if it exploded a mile up, there won't even be a shockwave, or fallout, really. It's dust from the ground that makes fallout."

Instinctively, he pulled his phone from his pocket to check the time again but, of course, it was dead. "Fuck, we need to go."

Just as he reached for the door handle, it opened from the other side. It was Ray, eyes bugged and breathing fast.

"Dude, is this a pulse?" He was wiping sweat from his forehead with a piece of toilet paper.

"I'm afraid so. Do you need to grab anything?"

"No, everything I need is in my Jeep. Let's go."

Ray was already running down the stairs with Rick and Angela following right behind him.

"Listen, Ray, Angela wants to come with us." Rick looked back at the woman following them down the steps who was nodding in response.

"I don't give a rat's ass if you bring her, but you're going to be responsible for her. My plan does not include anything but getting home to Sherry and Max."

Moving quickly down the stairs, he yelled at the couple over his shoulder, "Come on, we need to get out of here before everyone else figures out how fucked they really are."

By the fifth floor, the stairwell was starting to fill with people heading down toward the lobby. It was strangely quiet except for a couple of rowdy smokers who were vocally celebrating a chance to slip outside, burn a few, and shoot the shit.

TWO

As the trio reached the exit at the first floor, Ray broke the silence. "Let's try your car first, Rick. Where are you parked?"

"The same place I always park, remember? I get here early. I get any spot I want."

They went through the doors together and turned right toward the parking garage. Rick's car was parked on this level, so they took a moment to see if it would start. He pulled his keys from his pocket as they reached the blue Honda and pushed the unlock button on his key fob.

"It's not working."

"I expected as much, but you should get in there and try to start it to be sure."

Ray stood near the driver side as his brother put his key in the door to unlock it manually.

"Here goes." Climbing into the driver seat, Rick turned the key and there was nothing, not even a click from a dead battery. "Fucking hell! I still owe three years of payments on this piece of shit."

"I didn't expect it to work, did you?" Ray smiled and reached his hand out to pull his brother from the car. "Let's try the battle wagon."

His Jeep was an older model. Ray had once told Rick that it was a '72, manufactured before computers were installed in cars. When they reached the third floor of the parking garage, it was hard to miss. The camouflaged paint was splashed with mud from a weekend outing. Even though the body was murky brown, the wheels were spotless. Ray hated to drive around with dirt on his custom rims.

"Okay, let's try this baby." He climbed behind the wheel and stepped on the clutch. "Cross your fingers, Angela. Gimme some luck."

Ray held his breath and turned the key. Except for the clicking, nothing happened. He made a face and tried again. Still, there was nothing.

"Shit. I was afraid of that."

"What?" Angela was trembling. She was beginning to grasp the seriousness of their situation.

"The battery's dead. I've been having problems with it all week. Let's hope it's that. We'll try to push start it. If we can get it rolling..."

Reaching around, he pulled a canvas mailbag from beneath the cushion on the back seat and dropped it on the passenger side floor. It landed with an unusually heavy thunk for a bag made of cloth.

"Get ready, guys. First, I'm gonna need you to push it out of the space, then we'll try to take advantage of the ramp to get it going."

Rick went immediately to the front of the Jeep.

"C'mon, Angie."

She looked at her shoes with their high heels and shook her head. "I hate these damn shoes."

Slipping them off, she tossed them on the seat and joined Rick at the front of the vehicle. On Ray's "go," they started to push.

"Aaarrrrrrrrrgggggghhhhh! Is your foot on the brake, man? This thing is heavier than it looks." Rick was gritting his teeth and pushing, but the thing only moved a couple of feet. Angie's stocking covered feet were slipping on the smooth concrete and it was doubtful that she could offer any real help.

"Hey, you guys goin' somewhere?" A voice boomed from behind the vehicle.

Ray turned to see Drew walking in their direction. He was a big guy. If he was up for helping, he was just what they needed right now.

"We need to roll this thing out and push it over to the ramp to kick-start it."

"We're getting outta Dodge before everything turns to shit out there." Rick wiped his hands on his khakis. "We think the power outage was caused by…"

"An EMP? Yeah, I think so too. This is fucking insane!" There was a strange grin on his face as he walked up to the front of the Jeep and put his hands on the hood. "Let's get out of here. I hate this shithole."

The vehicle started to move on his first push and, when Rick and Angela joined in the effort, it rolled right out of the parking space. Ray turned the wheel as they put everything into it. They had to get the Jeep all the way around the deck to the other side to get to the down ramp. Finally reaching the sloping concrete, Ray popped the clutch and the Jeep roared to life, blowing a large cloud of black smoke out of the tailpipe.

"Damn! Is this thing gonna make it?" Rick coughed on the fumes.

"No worries, bro." He displayed his pearly whites in a huge grin. "Hop in. We're outta here in 60 seconds."

Rick and Angela climbed in the back, while Drew took shotgun. Ray revved the engine and threw the Jeep in gear making everyone lurch forward. Two more turns and they crashed through the gate arm, headed for the highway.

"I ruined my panty hose and my shoes. You really need to clean this thing out." Angela was holding up one of her red pumps and examining some new scratches close to the toe. "I hope I can find another pair at the mall. I really liked these."

Drew had no patience for her fashion concerns. He whirled around to confront her. "Girl, you obviously have no concept of what all of this means. We've just been kicked back to the Stone Age, and this here is the only horse in town. If we're lucky, we'll get to somewhere safe before the whole damned world comes apart. I don't think this is over yet."

Angie's tears began to well and Rick tried to soothe her. "We're going to Ray's place. He's been preparing for a day like this for years, right bro?"

Ray was nodding.

"See? We'll be alright if we can just get there."

Drew gave the driver a playful shove and asked, "Ray-Ray, you a prepper? Fuck, I knew it. You got a piece in that bag?"

"Two. Get 'em out."

Swerving past some stalled cars in the street, he turned the Jeep toward the freeway ramp.

Drew reached into the bag and pulled out a 9mm and a handful of loaded clips. "Yippie-ki-yay, motherfucker! Now we're talking!"

Rick held onto the roll bar and leaned forward. "You aren't taking the freeway are you?"

"Hell yeah, I am. There will be cars stalled all over. I can cruise right down the side of the road in the grass. We'll be there in twenty."

Ray slowed to make the turn onto the ramp. "There's another one in there. Get 'em loaded, Drew."

Drew pulled the second gun from the bag and slapped a clip into both.

"Locked and loaded. Here you go, Ricardo."

He handed one of the guns back to Rick and shouted, "You take care of anything coming up from behind, I got the front, and we'll both watch the sides."

"Do you think there is gonna be trouble?" Angela eyeballed the chrome-plated gun in his hand, not sure she liked the way things were going.

"Not at first, but the further we go the more desperate people might be for a ride. Everyone will want to get home to their families. That's how we survive," Rick replied.

A few people stood on the ramp next to their cars. They appeared dumbfounded, looking around as though they expected help to arrive any minute. Some had still not given up on their phones and were poking at them hoping they might come back on. The number of cars stranded at the bottom of the ramp was sobering.

"Holy shit!" Rick yelled as Ray swerved into the grass on the right side of the road and the ride got bumpy. "Slow down, man. You're gonna run somebody over."

Ray slowed and tried to keep his voice low. "Look, guys, if things get bad, I may actually have to run somebody down."

The sound of an explosion rumbled from behind them.

"What the fuck was that?" Angela pointed at something flying above the cars behind them, flipping and spinning in the air as it came toward them. In seconds, it was joined by several more.

"What the hell are you guys looking at back there?" Ray yelled over his shoulder as he swerved around a car that had rolled farther off the road than most.

"Oh shit!" Drew got his first look at them now. "There's some kind of drones or something, big fuckers shaped like, well, like flying pods from what I can tell."

He held his hand up to shield his eyes from the bright morning sunlight. "Holy fuck, something like cables, no, more like tentacles, just came out of its side and its grabbing people up right off of the road!"

Ray checked the rear view mirror just as one of the pods, now loaded down with people, jerked up and shot toward the clouds above.

"Fucking drive, Ray. One is coming right for us!" Angela was moving to get down onto the floor as the craft came up on them.

At least a half-dozen people were hanging from the tentacles on each side. When it swooped up, a little girl fell away from it and crashed through the windshield of one of the stalled cars. Everyone nearby screamed and scattered and Ray was having trouble navigating through them.

"Hold on, I have to get away from the highway."

He swerved sharply and got up over the bank crashing through the chain link fence. The Jeep settled among some pine trees and sputtered as though it was going to stall.

"No, baby, don't die on us now!"

He shifted it to neutral and revved the engine to keep it running, then backed off the accelerator and pulled the hand brake. The tall pines formed a canopy above them, and they were hidden from the road by the hill they had crossed.

"We need to figure out what the hell we are up against here."

Ray jumped out of the Jeep and crept back toward the highway to check out the situation. Rick and Drew looked at each other and climbed out to follow Ray.

"Wait here, Angie."

"Don't worry. I'm not going anywhere," she replied as she got out, rolled under the vehicle and slipped out of view.

J. H. Glaze

THREE

The men hid in the tall grass, sprawling out on the bank looking over the ridge. From there, they could see the chaos that was unfolding on the highway. Men, women and children ran in all directions while the aliens gathered them up like farm workers picking vegetables. When every tentacle had seized a human captive, the pods would swoop up into the clouds laden with screaming people.

"This is some horrible shit. There's gotta be something we can do," Rick whispered to his brother, his voice nearly drowned out by the screaming people below.

"There's not a fucking thing we can do right now except wait. We are way outnumbered and probably outgunned."

Ray gasped as one of the pods grabbed at a woman, missed and caught her by the hair, ripping it from her scalp like a cheap wig. She screamed and clutched at her bloody head before she passed out.

"Motherfuckers!" Drew yelled out. He was moving to go to the woman's aid when Rick grabbed hold of his belt.

"Let go of me, bitch! I'm going to take some action, not sit here like *you* pussy asses, and there's nothing you can do about it."

He squeezed the grip of his gun, but stopped himself from using it to threaten Rick. His knuckles were white from the vise-like grip he had on the piece.

"Easy, bud. I just don't want you to get yourself killed. We need your help to get to Ray's place. After that, you can split if you want. Go save the planet."

Rick was trying to defuse the situation, just as another pod swept down and began rounding up more people.

"If there's any planet left to save," Ray mumbled as once again his eyes turned to the horror before them.

For at least a half hour, the abductions continued until that part of the highway was nearly clear. Most of the people left standing there were senior citizens. Ray had a thought about why that might be.

"Hey, did either of you see those things grab any of the older folks?"

"What? No, I don't remember seeing any. Now that you mention it, they took the rest of the people that were standing all around them. The older ones were left behind." Rick could see an elderly couple making their way to the woods about twenty yards away.

"So the fuckers are scanning for AARP cards? I guess membership has its benefits," Drew wisecracked. "Sorry. I can't watch any more of this shit."

He pushed himself up from the bank and turned to walk back to the Jeep. When the brothers stood to follow, they saw Angela sitting in the front seat and talking to a skinny guy with red curly hair. As they got closer, the shotgun he was holding came into view. There was another leaning against the Jeep. The guy turned to face them, they could make out the twin bandoleers of shotgun shells he wore crisscrossing his chest.

"Hola!" Drew quipped, "Where's your sombrero, hombre?"

"Nice to know people can still have a sense of humor when the world around them has gone to hell," the stranger returned. "Where's your Santa suit? Oh wait, Santa has *white* hair and a beard, doesn't he?"

"If you guys are done auditioning for the comedy club, we need to get our asses in gear while the getting is good," Ray said. "What's your name, dude? Is it okay if we call you dude?"

"Dude is cool with me as long as you put THE in front of it, but no, my name's Greg." He pretended to tip an invisible sombrero.

"Nice to meet somebody else with guns. We might have a better chance than those poor bastards did." He waved his shotgun in the direction of the highway. "What say we get rolling?"

"Say what?"

"Yeah, I remember a scene in Dune where Muad'dib met the Fremen. They captured him until…"

"Fucker uses a scene from Dune as an example? He's cool." Drew motioned the guy to climb into the Jeep.

"Easy for you to say, Drew. You got the front seat." Rick wasn't thrilled about adding another body to the team.

"Look, I don't want to be a burden." Greg grabbed his second shotgun and turned to leave.

"Hang on, Greg." Ray glared at his brother. "We could use some extra fire power."

The carrot top turned back and smiled. "Hey, I'll stand and hold onto the roll bar if I have to. At least you guys have wheels, and I do *not* feel like walking today."

FOUR

The going was slow on this part of the highway. It was a creepy scene with abandoned cars as far as they could see. The median was rough and they were lucky to reach five miles per hour.

"You think they took all of these people?" Angela twirled her hair nervously as she looked around at the wrecks and empty vehicles.

"Except for the old ones, I'm guessing." Rick looked straight ahead, checking for gaps between the cars big enough for the Jeep to fit through.

"Maybe surface streets would be better. We should try the next exit," Drew suggested as he shifted in his seat trying to get comfortable. "The clouds have cleared over there, and... Hey, check this out! There's the ship up there, and it's huge! There's a helluva lot of room for us cattle in that thing."

"Shit! Fucking thing's gotta be over a mile long!" Rick said. He squinted as the sun reflected off the gleaming ship. Even though it was blocking the sun, the glare against the metal lit up the scene around them like a giant mirror.

21

"Yeah, well let me know if you see any of those drones headed our way." Ray snaked his way through a line of tractor-trailers that had died.

"How do you know they're drones?" Greg hadn't had much to say since they had gotten back on the road. "Drone implies that there's no pilot inside. It's possible that something or someone is flying them."

"Is that from a scene in Dune, too?" Rick jabbed.

"No, not really. The Hunter-Seekers in Dune were drones. They were unmanned because they were too small to...."

"I give up. Ray, are you taking the next exit?"

"Surface streets are the long way home, man. I'd rather take a straighter route."

Drew offered his two cents. "Yeah, but there's no traffic lights, and if it isn't as crowded, it might be quicker. We can drive on the sidewalk if we have to."

"True." Ray didn't really care to debate their route at the moment. All he could think of was his wife and son. Would they even be there, or would they have gone to one of the neighbor's houses looking for help until he got back home? It tore at his heart to think they might have been carried away by one of those things while he wasn't there to protect them.

"There." He spotted the exit ahead and began winding his way through the cars toward it.

"Hey, you know what really sucks?" Drew looked disappointed. "I just got the new *Blades of the Forgotten World* video game last night. Didn't even take the plastic wrapper off. Now I might never get to play it. I heard it was cutting edge awesomeness." Even though it was a stupid thing to say, it seemed a good idea to offer a diversion rather than more doom and gloom.

Rick cut him some slack. He knew Drew loved video games and always enjoyed talking about them. In fact, Rick had been planning on doing some intense gaming himself. Only weeks before, he had made the change to an eighty-inch television. He even paid extra to have it wall mounted and purchased a state of the art sound system to match, but after today, it wasn't worth a can of soda. Likely, he would never be able to sit on his black leather sofa and enjoy it again.

Rick had been watching the road ahead. "Hey, guys, I was just thinking…"

Just as they reached the top of the off ramp and turned to cross the overpass, he saw masses of people crowding the street. It was obvious that some had abandoned their cars on the highway. They were being herded into a tightly condensed group by enormous robot-like creatures, which now completely blocked the road.

"Turn around, Ray. Do it now." Drew was standing up in the Jeep to get a better look. "It looks like a cattle drive, but them ain't no cowboys. They're more like Mechs, kinda like those Japanese Manga toys."

"You mean Transformers?" Angie pulled some glasses from the small purse she had stashed in the Jeep earlier.

"No," Drew answered. "Those definitely are not Bumblebee or Optimus Prime. They look a lot more menacing, and no one in that crowd is trying to challenge them"

Ray had just started to pass around a large truck when a group of men charged one of the Mechs. He could see them closing in on it, but the thing was considerably faster. All of a sudden, it shot into the sky leaving the men below to collide.

Before they could recover their footing, it was falling back to earth. It landed hard, crushing everyone beneath it into a crimson shower of gore that rained down on all nearby. The terrified cry of the crowd went out in an echoing scream.

Ray dodged cars, turned the Jeep around and sped off in the other direction as his passengers turned back to watch what would happen next. Would anyone be brave enough to rush those things again? They would never find out. Ray punched it and swerved around a delivery truck, shooting down the road and away from the slaughter that was about to commence.

J. H. Glaze

FIVE

Awed by the show of force, they slowly traveled the road in silence for the next few miles. There were no people to be seen. No one running for cover, no one standing in shock. There were cars smashed and on fire. It was obvious that something had happened here.

"Why are they taking people? This doesn't make sense." Angie's voice was shaky. Her makeup streaked down her face making her look like a character from a low budget horror film.

"People used to think that if aliens came, they would be after our resources. Remember the sci-fi show, "V"? Aliens pretended to come here for chemical waste that was needed for their planet, but what they really wanted was our water and to use us for... well, for food." Greg shrugged and added, "I could believe it's food they're after."

"They could have raided the damn grocery stores. Fuckers too lazy to stand in line?" Drew sat back and tried to think of some painful kind of retaliation they could visit on the bastards.

Ray pulled off the road under some trees and yanked the parking brake. "We need a plan. If we run into another one of those roundups, we need to be prepared to get through it."

"Or, to stop it," Rick added.

"Any ideas?" Ray stepped out to check the tires on the Jeep. He had driven through quite a lot of broken glass and twisted metal parts. Aside from running out of gas, a couple of flat tires were about the only thing that could keep him from getting home. "Nobody?"

"We have the guns and that's about it." Rick wasn't sure how much ammo they had, but he hoped it would be enough until they could get some more at Ray's house.

"Right, well then, here's my plan." Ray climbed back in the driver seat and turned to the others. "If we come up on one of those cluster fucks, that is if we spot it in time, we should try to find a way to go around it without getting caught up in it. Without better weapons, we can't save anybody. Maybe not even ourselves."

He put the Jeep in gear and steered back out into the open, down the wide sidewalk as far as he could until forced to get back on the street.

"How far from the house are we now?" Rick asked his brother.

"Not sure. I never measured it going this way, but if I had to guess, I'd say about five to seven miles."

Drew put his hand on Ray's shoulder. "Hey, be quiet and listen."

"Jet?" Greg cupped his hand around his ear trying to hear.

It was seconds before they located the military jet fighter and four pods in pursuit. The jet began to pull up in a steep climb as explosives were released behind it. Puffs of smoke surrounded the alien craft as each one hit its mark. There was a lag before they could hear the sound of the explosion.

"Go, man! Blow those bastards out of the sky!" Drew yelled, shaking his fist at the scene.

The pods appeared unaffected by the blasts and continued to gain on the jet. Two of them separated from the formation and suddenly shot ahead of the fighter as the pilot launched a missile toward them.

Again, it seemed as though there was hope. The missile's release brought a cheer from the group, but it was short-lived. The missile appeared to reverse its flight path and flew straight back into the fighter. With a burst of fire, the jet was vaporized.

"What just happened?" Ray had been keeping his eyes on the road in front of him and had only seen the flash in his rearview mirror. "Guys?"

"It's fucking gone. They deflected the missile right back at it. Pieces are falling from the sky." Drew sat back into his seat. "We're so screwed."

Ray's heart sank. If the Air Force couldn't stop even one of those things, whatever the aliens were planning for the rest of them was sure to play out to a terrifying conclusion.

Greg muttered under his breath before he yelled out loud, "Drive, Ray! Drive! Drive! Drive! One of those fucking things is coming right at us."

Ray pushed the gas pedal hard, but he was still dodging cars and wasn't able to go much faster. He heard the sound of the shotgun as Greg racked a shell in the chamber.

"Get ready!"

Drew pulled the slide back on the 9mm and checked to make sure there was a shell in the chamber. He reached up to grip the roll bar so he could stand while he fired. The thing was already hovering over the Jeep, its metal tentacles thrashing, trying to get hold of anyone inside.

Greg pulled the shotgun back and fired a shot directly into the center of its underside. The blast was enough to knock it away a few feet, but it had managed to wrap one of its tentacles around Drew.

"Oh shit, it's got me!" he shrieked. "Do something!"

The pod started to pull up, but without a counterbalance on the opposite side, Drew's weight pulled it down on one side. It was slow to move away. The others wanted to fire, but were afraid of hitting Drew. They could hear him yelling and cursing, but felt helpless to do anything about it.

As the pod began to rise, Drew pulled at the tentacle that was wrapped around his body but was unable to free himself from it. There was an electric shock coming from it that made it difficult to keep his grip.

About twenty feet off the ground, the pod began flying away toward the mother ship. It was then that he realized he was still holding the gun in his hand. He grabbed the tentacle and this time pulled up closer to the metallic body.

Once close enough, he placed the muzzle of the pistol against the base of the tentacle. Firing through the base into the body of the craft, he screamed in defiance. "Fuck you, you piece of shit!"

The pod was flying over a construction site when the tentacle lost its hold on Drew, dropping him into a large mound of sand. The craft flipped, wobbled and crashed into the metal frame of a partially completed building. It hung there for a moment before dropping to the ground. Thrashing about, with tentacles flying, it disintegrated in a blinding flash of light.

Drew pushed himself up from the sand, and for a moment, he wasn't sure what had just happened. As he shook himself off, he did a clumsy victory dance, yelling, "Yeah, bitch! I beat you, motherfucker!" The Jeep pulled up next to him, and he nearly fell in front of it.

"Hey, man, if you are done celebrating, we need to get the hell outta here." Rick smiled and offered him a hand to climb back into his seat.

SIX

It was a frantic few miles to Ray's house as they took side streets and dodged several roundups of people who had wandered out into the open. Each time they saw a group being culled from the street, they could hear them screaming like animals being forced into a slaughterhouse.

When they finally pulled into his driveway, Ray jumped out to run into the house. Instinctively, he took the keys out of the ignition.

"I'll be right back," he shouted over his shoulder. "If they're not in there, we're going to have to search for them."

The others got out to stretch and waited next to the vehicle. Even if Ray's family was there, they figured he would want a minute alone with them before having his house overrun by strangers.

"I hope they're okay in there. It would suck to come all this way and find nobody at home, or worse." Angie covered her mouth to keep herself from finishing her thought.

Drew had to agree. "It would be the ultimate hose job to go through all of that for nothing. Otherwise, we could have found shelter somewhere along the way."

He rubbed his arm where a large welt was forming. "When that thing grabbed me – it wasn't just the squeeze, there was some kind of sting, like a stun gun. Hurt like hell."

"If Ray has food and more guns and ammo, that would make the trip worth it, now wouldn't it?" Greg leaned back against the Jeep. Ray had parked it under the trees next to his driveway for cover, so the group didn't have to be concerned about being seen from above.

"Yeah, I guess you could say it's lucky Ray's been a prepper for years. I'm kind of surprised he brought us all here. He always talked about what he would do if some shit came down, but it never seemed like he was keen on including anyone else. Not even me."

Rick didn't sound upset about it. After all, they were here now. His brother must have modified his strategy on the fly. Meanwhile, no one saw the fully loaded gas tanker falling from the sky. Angie screamed as it crushed Ray's house and exploded in flames.

"Holy shit!" Drew looked up through the branches overhead and saw six pods. They hovered above them and appeared to be identical to the one he had brought down.

"Looks like they've found us, and I think they're fucking pissed."

Greg stopped Rick, who was about to run toward the house. "There's nothing you can do, man, and if you run out in the open, those things will grab you."

"Ray!" Rick sounded desperate. "Let go of me! That's my fucking brother in there. I can't just stand here and watch."

Suddenly, Ray, along with his wife and son, were hauling ass through the gate to his back yard.

"Get in the Jeep, now!" Ray yelled as he came toward them.

No one hesitated. Everyone got into the Jeep, and Ray helped his wife into Drew's lap. He handed his son to Rick before he jumped behind the wheel.

"Do *not* let them get him, bro. I'm counting on you."

"I got this. Just drive."

Ray turned the key in the ignition and the engine groaned as it tried to turn over.

"You shouldn't have shut the fucking thing off!" Angie yelled in a panic.

The engine cranked again and it started. Ray slammed the Jeep into gear. With the pedal to the metal, it shot out from under the trees. They jumped a hill that separated his yard from the neighbors and headed straight across several well-manicured lawns before attempting to get back to the street. Two sharp turns and they were back on the pavement and picking up speed.

"Drive on the sidewalk, Ray. When you were cutting through the yards, they couldn't get so close to us because of the trees. Now they're closing in again." Rick held five-year old Max to the floor with his legs and braced himself with the roll bar to keep both of them from bouncing out. "Go, go, go! Here they come."

One of the pods swooped down with its tentacles extended. It was making its move just as Ray swerved under a giant oak tree. The craft was unable to counter the move and slammed into the tree. There was no explosion as it wedged between two of the largest limbs.

"You got him!" Greg cheered and watched the tentacles thrash as the pod tried to free itself. "Like a rat in a trap. Circle back and let me finish it off."

"No can do. We need to keep going." Ray slowed the vehicle to drive through a large hedge.

Just before the impact, Greg jumped out. "Go ahead. I want to kill this one."

As he hit the ground, his legs went out from under him and he rolled a few feet.

"He's down!" Angie gasped. "Wait. He's okay. He's headed back to the tree."

"Fuck! I told him not to do that."

Ray considered whether he could circle back, but there wasn't enough space to turn the Jeep around.

***

Greg had second thoughts about his decision as he stood up from his rolling exit.

"Stupid, stupid, but fuck it, I'm in it now."

He picked up his shotgun and ran back to the oak tree. He didn't have far to go before he was standing beneath the pod. It looked much bigger hanging there above him. Raising his shotgun, he aimed it directly at the metal underbelly. He hesitated just long enough to eye his escape route in case the thing broke free, and then pulled the trigger.

The shot hit its mark, and a loud screeching noise came from somewhere inside the pod. He racked another shell and fired again at the same spot. The metallic skin burst open as he hit his mark again. A steaming fluid poured from it and splashed on the ground at his feet.

"What the fuck are you?" he yelled up as the screeching sound began to fade, racked another shell and fired again.

Whatever the answer, the other pods were headed toward him in response to the call. They were on him before he knew it, and he was surrounded. There was no way to run in any direction. They had him dead to rights.

Racking another shell as fast as he could, Greg pointed the shotgun at the pod directly in front of him. He pulled the trigger and click. The shell was a misfire.

Faster than he could react, the pods whipped out their tentacles and grabbed him. In the blink of an eye, his body was pulled apart, his arms and legs were ripped away.

A tentacle from another pod seized Greg's bleeding torso. Taking its trophy, it shot up to the sky as the remaining pods dropped the other body parts in the grass and followed. The lifeless pod that had hung from the tree disappeared in a bright flash, and the branches that had held it fell to the ground.

SEVEN

"Does anybody see the aliens? We're almost there." Ray was watching the skies and trying to stay under the trees as much as possible.

"I can't see the one that was stuck in the tree anymore, Daddy." Max was kneeling on Drew's lap and holding onto the top of the windshield. "It's not there. Is it dead?"

"Where's Greg? I don't see him either." Angie was leaning to see around the boy.

At first, there was no sign of Greg anywhere, but then Rick saw what appeared to be a shirtsleeve with an arm still attached to it. "Turn around, Ray. He's gone." He put his hand on his brother's shoulder and leaned forward to whisper in his ear. "They tore him apart, poor bastard."

"Damn, he was a good guy." Ray turned the wheel and headed off in the opposite direction.

"We didn't even look for him," Angie protested through tears. "How do you know he's gone?"

"Angie, do you really want to know what happened to him?" Drew turned his head to look at her and saw her vacant expression.

39

"Right, I know this really sucks, but we have to push past it."

"Fuck you, Drew." She almost spat at him.

"That's right! Get it all out." He smiled.

"Where are we headed, Ray?" It was the first Sherry had spoken since seeing her home go up in flames. "Obviously, we aren't going home. Everything we worked so hard for... gone in an instant. We don't even have clothes."

"Everything will be okay, honey. We can do this. We've done it before."

"Not like this, Ray," Sherry sobbed.

Defeat weighed on Ray's soul. It wasn't easy to shake it off, and he drove in complete silence. Glancing at the faces of his family and friends in the rearview mirror, he realized that for the first time in his life, he didn't have a plan. The uncertainty made him feel sick to his stomach.

"Look over there, Ray." Rick pointed at the entrance to a parking deck beneath the community hospital. "Let's use the cover of the garage and figure this out."

Ray didn't reply. Driving to the entrance, he crashed straight through the dropped gate without stopping to lift it. There was a loud bang as the metal gate struck the hood of the Jeep and snapped off. He turned to go down another level before he pulled into a parking spot and shifted to neutral.

"Come on," Ray said. "We can leave it running for a minute to make sure the battery stays charged. Let's find someplace quiet."

Once out of the vehicle, he led the group back up the ramp. He had been to this hospital before, and he knew that the only way up from the parking deck was by elevator or on foot. At the top and to the right of the ramp there were double glass doors that led into the main lobby and reception area.

The automatic doors were not responding with the power off, so Ray and Drew forced them open. Turning to check behind them for any imminent danger, everyone filed into the building.

***

The lobby of the hospital was abandoned, but there were signs all around that people had left in a hurry. Magazines and papers were scattered across the floor and scuttled about in the breeze from the open doors.

"Where do you think everyone went?" Sherry asked as she sat down in one of the chairs in the waiting area and leaned forward to rest her face in her hands.

"Probably tried to get home to their families. I wonder if any of them made it." Ray sat next to his wife and rubbed her shoulder, trying to relieve some of the stress.

"So, if the workers left, what do you suppose happened to the patients?" Drew scanned the mess on the reception desk.

"Let's go find out." Ray got up and started down the hall. "We need supplies anyway. We can search for what we need while we check around for anyone still here. Rick, you take Angie and Drew and find the cafeteria while we go up to the second floor."

"Wait a second, Ray. Here's a floor map. Second floor is Pediatrics. I guess that's a good place for you guys to start." Rick took another look at the map. "I see the cafeteria here. I'd tell you to meet us back here in fifteen minutes, but there's no way for us to tell time, so don't be too long or we'll have to look for you."

"No worries. We'll make it quick."

Ray stepped over to the floor map and found the way to the main stairwell. He took hold of Max's hand, and Sherry reached for his other one. He led them down the hall to the stairs. Before opening the door, he stopped and squatted down to talk directly to Max.

"Hey, bud. I don't know what we're going to find in there. It could be bad, you know. Are you ready to handle it if there's something bad, little man?"

The boy looked him in the eyes and whispered, "What kinda bad stuff, Dad?"

"Well, I can't be sure, son."

"Like what happened to that other guy? His leg was on the ground by itself. It was gross."

Ray hesitated and looked up at Sherry before answering. "Yeah, maybe like that."

"It's okay, Dad. I see stuff like that on TV."

"Huh?"

Sherry butted in. "Ray, I told you to be selective about what you watch with him. He doesn't miss a thing."

"Don't worry, Mom. These guys aren't zombies. Dad can handle them. Right, Dad?"

"Right. No zombies, we're good." Ray rubbed his son's head and stood to open the door. The stairwell was dark and smelled musty as they stepped into it.

J. H. Glaze

EIGHT

Rick was in the cafeteria kitchen where the reflection of light from the hallway bounced off the stainless steel equipment. "Do you see a stockroom?" he asked the others.

"That door over there is either a walk-in cooler or a freezer." Drew walked over and pulled the handle to yank open the door. He half expected to see someone hiding in there but was relieved to find that the only thing inside was food. He pulled a lighter from his pocket and used it to look around.

"What's in there?" Angie stayed behind him in case something jumped out from the darkness.

"Nothing but lettuce, milk and shit like that. There's probably some meat here, too. We could make ourselves something to eat with this stuff, but we can't take it with us. It would just rot. I say we have lunch."

"I don't know how you can think about eating right now," Angie scoffed.

"No really, Angie. Look at me. You think I got this amazing man body from starving myself? I'm hungry as fuck right now."

"Hey, guys," Rick called. "I found food. It's not the best survival food, but we could live off it for a while. There's a rack of sandwich rolls, and a lot of canned food. I found a cart, so help me load it up."

"Rick, really, man? A cart? We came here in a Jeep. There are six of us counting Ray's kid." Drew was in the cooler now looking for something to pull out for lunch. "Where are we gonna put a cart full of food?"

"Fuck, you're right. Why do you always have to be right, Drew?"

"In this case, I find no satisfaction in being right." He reached down to grab something. "Aha! Rib-eye steaks! They must save these for the doctors. I never saw that at the steam table before. These look just like my lunch."

Angie stepped in to look for something she might want. "How are you gonna cook with the power out?"

In response to her question, Drew walked straight out of the cooler and over to the grill. As soon as he threw the handful of steaks on it, they began to sizzle. "Grills are heated with gas. I figured they'd still be hot."

***

Ray was trying to see through the wire-reinforced glass in the door to the second floor.

He was checking to make sure that nothing was lurking on the other side. What he saw crushed his spirit, nearly bringing him to tears.

"Oh God, there are kids left in there."

He turned the handle and pulled the door open. As Sherry and Max followed him out of the darkness, his dread increased as he realized that there were dozens of children wandering the hallway. Some of them appeared to be in pretty bad shape.

A little girl was moving toward them. "Hey, we saw monsters outside. Everyone was screaming. Are there soldiers with you?"

Max answered first as he stood face to face with the girl who was wrapped in a white hospital bathrobe. "My dad and uncle are here. They're better than Army guys." He straightened with pride as he spoke.

The girl did not take comfort in his answer. Her face contorted as she began to cry. Sherry stooped to hug the little girl, holding her close as the tears continued.

"We're here to help. It's gonna be okay." She was lying, of course. She did not believe that things were going to end well, but she didn't know what else to say. More children had gathered out in the hall, all of them in various states of poor health. It was easy to read the fear in their faces.

"Dad, can we take them with us? They can come with us, right?"

"I don't know, Max. All we have is the Jeep, and we hardly fit in it as it is." He spoke quietly so as not to scare the others.

In the hallway, Ray looked over each child as Sherry and Max checked the rooms. In every room that was still occupied, Sherry would find another child who was unable to leave their bed on their own. At the end of the hall, she turned to look back at Ray and shook her head.

"Some of the kids can't walk, and I think a few have died already." The voice of a teen-aged boy made him jump. He spun to see who was behind him.

"Oh, man, you scared the shit out of me."

"Sorry, sir. I didn't mean…" The boy looked down at the floor.

Ray put his hand on his shoulder. "Hey, its all right. I'm just jittery after what's been going on out there. How many kids do you think are on this floor?"

"Maybe thirty. Like I said, some died already, mostly the ones who were on machines. They went quick after the power went out."

"Are most of the kids pretty sick, or… why are you here?"

"I was having pain in my stomach. The doctor said I had to have surgery. It was supposed to be this morning."

"Well, you look okay now." Ray was beginning to feel uncomfortable.

"I don't know, it sucks. They said I have cancer. The way they talked, I needed surgery right away. Now I guess it won't happen."

"Where are your parents?"

"I don't know. The nurses took me into a room to get me ready and said they would be right back, but nobody came back. I was looking for them when I found all of these other kids."

Ray didn't want the young man to see his tears. He was desperate to come up with a plan of action.

"I'd better go downstairs to see what the others have found. Please tell my wife and son I'll be right back."

He was headed toward to the stairwell before the boy could answer.

J. H. Glaze

NINE

When Ray got to the hospital kitchen, he found the rest of the group feasting on steak and fries.

"I see you guys found food."

Drew had to finish chewing before he could speak.

"Yeah, there's a lot of food here, but most of it is either in the cooler or the freezer. It's going to go bad, so we decided to eat some. What did you find?" Angie cut another bite of steak as she spoke.

"A floor full of kids."

Drew spit the bite out of his mouth. "How many?"

"There was a teenage kid up there who said he counted about thirty. It really sucks, but I guess we'll need to stay here."

"Man, that's fucked up. We can't stay here." Rick turned away from the counter where he was making a sandwich. Suddenly, he had lost his appetite.

Ray pointed at the food the others had piled up. "It looks like we have food. We can hang out here for a while until the aliens move on."

"And what if they don't move on?" Angie had stopped eating.

"I don't think we have much of a choice. There's no way the Jeep can hold everybody *and* the food." Rick said, as he walked to the door and looked out into the hallway.

"What if we had a bus?" Angie held her hands up to illustrate a longer vehicle. "Could we go then?

"Sure, if we had a bus, but we don't," Ray replied.

"I think there were some buses not far from here. There was a church in that last block before we got here, and I'm pretty sure there were a couple of buses parked behind it."

Drew swallowed. "If we had a bus, we could load it up. Kids and food, that could work. What do you think, Ray? Those church buses are usually old, but I don't doubt we could get one running."

"It's possible, but we have to get there first."

"Let's go then." It was the teenager from the children's ward. He was standing in the doorway. "I'll help. What do you need me to do?"

Drew answered, "What's your name, kid?"

"Michael. Mike."

"Well, Michael Mike, you could start by helping us look for some bandages, medicine, shit like that."

"Just Mike. Is that food?"

"Yeah, you hungry?"

"Yes, sir. What do you have?" The boy moved into the kitchen to see what they were eating.

Ray had an idea. "Angie, I need you to go back upstairs to the kids' rooms and gather the charts. Maybe we can find the medicine they need around here somewhere. Ask my wife to help you, and tell her we are going to get a bus."

"She asked me to tell you something. That's why I came down." Mike interrupted before taking the bite from the sandwich Rick had given him.

"What did she say?"

"She said for you to find a way to get everyone out of here, but it looks like you already did that." He smiled and took the bite.

"Yes, we're gonna make this work. We have no other option."

TEN

In the lower level of the parking deck, Ray and Drew stood beside the stalled Jeep.

"If it doesn't start, we're fucked. I don't think it ran out of gas." Ray kicked a tire and then climbed into the driver seat.

"I don't know, man." Drew stretched his back. "I might be able to push it again. I'm sore, but not that sore."

"Here goes." Ray climbed into the driver seat and put the key in the ignition. The engine started on the first try. "Hell yeah! Get in."

Drew did as told and climbed into the passenger seat. "When we get to the entrance, stop and let me check to make sure it's clear before you pull out. I'd hate like hell to cruise right out into the open and get grabbed by one of those pod things... again."

The Jeep rolled slowly through the parking deck, up to the exit arm and stopped. Ray turned to Drew. "Are you sure you want to get out and look, or do you want me to do it. I understand if..."

"Naw, man, I got this."

Drew swung his legs out of the Jeep and walked carefully up to the exit. He took a deep breath and cautiously leaned out into the open to look around before taking a step out. He made a complete turn to check the sky. Climbing back into his seat, he reported, "Coast is clear."

Ray shifted into gear and slowly drove against the drop arm of the deck until it snapped. He pulled out onto the drive and headed for the street.

"We're going to backtrack, so watch for that church."

The two were silent as they rolled past the same buildings they had seen earlier.

"Over there." Drew pointed. "Old ass buses."

Ray turned the wheel and pulled into the church parking lot. There were two blue buses parked side by side. Each was painted with the words, "Jesus Saves," and "First Church of Christ," in bright yellow letters. He drove up to the nearest bus.

"Let's check them out. Look for keys under the visor. I wouldn't think they would worry about these old buses being stolen. Seems like that would be a burn-in-hell offense for sure." With that, Ray disappeared through the door of the first bus.

Drew did the same, climbing clumsily into the driver seat of the second bus. It was a tight fit for a guy his size. Reaching up, he pulled the visor and a set of keys fell in his lap.

"Damn, just like in the movies," he muttered as he inserted the ignition key and turned it.

Click. Click.

Meanwhile, Ray was getting back into the driver seat of his bus. The keys had fallen to the floor and slid beneath the loose matting. Now he inserted the key, and looked up. "If you're there, now would be a good time to..." He turned the key and it started. "Well, thank you, Jesus!"

Drew heard the sound of the engine and abandoned his bus with the grace of a hippo on a tightrope. As he walked around the front of the running bus, he held his fists in the air as a sign of victory.

"I'll follow you back," he yelled at Ray and headed for the Jeep.

Ray pulled the bus forward and toward the street while Drew fell in behind, driving the four-wheeler with a huge grin on his face.

"I always wanted one of these babies." He reached down, shifted gears, and hit the gas to catch up with the bus.

ELEVEN

As Angie watched through the large glass windows of the reception area, she saw the bus heading for the covered drive. She squealed with delight and ran for the stairwell. By the time she reached the second floor, Sherry and Max were already herding the kids that could walk on their own toward the stairs.

"They got a bus!" Angie yelled as she burst through the door.

"We need help up here," Sherry called back. She was pushing a wheelchair into one of the rooms.

Max was leading the other children quietly down the hall and through the door to the stairwell. They wound down the stairs and out the door at the bottom where they found Ray just about to go up.

"Hey, buddy!" He hugged Max. "Take them out to the bus and help Drew get them settled in. Leave the last four seats empty for the food. I'm gonna go in and help your mom." He gave the boy another squeeze and released him.

"Let's get on the bus, guys." Max waved for the children to follow.

When they got to the bus, Max told Drew, "Dad said to leave the last four seats for food."

Drew helped each child up the steps. "Move to the back, and leave the last four seats empty." He repeated it to each one as he cautiously watched the sky for pods.

***

On the second floor, Angie and Sherry stood in the hall where three wheelchairs held half a dozen kids. These were children who were unable to walk on their own for one reason or another.

"What's up?" Ray found them talking together quietly.

"We're not sure what to do about the ones who can't be moved. They are still in their beds and a few are unconscious." Sherry's eyes were pleading. "We've already lost a few that were very sick. Some must have passed as soon as the power went out, poor babies."

"We don't have much choice here, Sherry. We can take the ones in the chairs, but anyone who goes in the bus has got to be mobile. We might have to abandon the bus at some point and make a run for it."

Ray looked around at the kids who were waiting to be moved. "I can't even guarantee that we will be able to protect them if we come under attack."

"He's right, Sherry. We didn't ask for this. We never expected to be in this situation. We can only do what we can do." Angie was carrying bags full of bandages and medicine. She hated to admit that Ray was right, but he was.

Ray gave her a nod of appreciation. "Let's get these kids downstairs. Drew and Rick are already loading the bus. We need to get on the road."

Taking hold of the handles of one of the wheelchairs, he pushed it toward the stairwell. The two women each got behind a wheelchair and followed. When he reached the door, he stopped and scooped up the two kids from the chair.

"Get the door for me. I'll be right back for the others."

He looked at the kids. "Ready?"

They nodded, and Sherry opened the door, allowing him to disappear down the stairwell. She continued holding the door open to let the light from the hallway spill into the darkness until she heard the door open below.

At the first floor, Ray asked one of kids to turn the handle on the door. Kicking the door open, he pushed through and carried the children to the front entrance that led to the bus.

Just then, Rick came up behind him. "I have all of the food sorted and loaded on a cart that I found near the loading dock. I think we have enough to last for a while."

As Ray turned toward him, Rick saw the two frightened children his brother was carrying. "Hey kids, don't worry. It's gonna be okay."

Ray was a little out of breath. "Move the cart out to the bus and get Drew to help you load it up. Hey, Drew, come take these kids and get them on the bus. There are four more to bring down. After you get these two situated, Rick's going to need some help."

"Sure. Anything else?"

"Yeah, did you grab some bread and milk? It can't be spoiled yet. We have to make it quick. We need to get out of here while the sky's still clear."

***

When Ray was back on the second floor, Sherry and Angie were ready to go. Max was doing a last sweep of the rooms.

"Max, I need you to go ahead and help Uncle Rick."

"Sure, Dad." Max stopped what he was doing and shot through the door.

Each woman was holding a child who was holding a small bag. Ray asked, "What's in the bags?"

"Medicine. The lists are in the bag for who needs what. We grabbed everything we could find."

Ray nodded and smiled at her, then took a child in each arm from the wheelchair and went back to the stairwell door. Just as Angie was about to open it for him, they heard crying coming from one of the rooms.

"Some of the kids were in such bad shape that there was no way we could move them." Angie pulled the door open. "We are saving as many as we can."

"Fuck, this sucks, but I agree." Ray shook his head and headed down the stairs with the two women behind him.

Sherry whispered in the darkness, "Honey, please, the language."

J. H. Glaze

TWELVE

Ray was helping the last of the kids find a seat when he saw Rick and Max pushing the cart piled high with boxes of food toward the doors.

"Let's load it through the back," Drew called to them. "Hey, do you think we should tie the kids down in there in case it gets rough? There aren't any seat belts."

The two pushed the cart to the back of the bus where Drew was trying to get the emergency door to open. He asked one of the kids to push the release bar from the inside to unlock it. A boy hit the bar, and the door flew open nearly knocking Drew on his ass. The door alarm began to blast its warning sound across the parking lot.

"Fuck me!" Drew scrambled to his feet and fumbled with the bar on the door. The bus was so high that he had to reach above his head. Before he could find a way to shut the alarm off, the battery died and it fell silent.

Rick stepped up into the bus and began searching for something to use to secure the kids in their seats. As the noise of the alarm quieted, he yelled back toward Drew, "There's nothing here to use for seatbelts. We're going to have to go without. How much more time do you need? That alarm might have gotten us some unwanted attention."

"Give me three more minutes."

Drew began lifting whole cases of cans though the door of the bus. "Max, I'm gonna lift you up. I need you and Rick to move this stuff up so I can get the rest of it in."

Before the boy could answer, he was being hoisted into the bus. Drew called out to the women, "Angie, Sherry, give them a hand to get this stuff loaded."

He continued hefting boxes and cans in the door. Within the three minutes he had requested, everything on the cart was loaded into the bus. The effort had left him gasping for breath and doubled over.

"Hey, big guy, are you alright? Close that door and drag your ass up here so we can go," Ray hollered toward the back of the bus.

"Sh... shit." Drew took another breath, slammed the back door of the bus and pushed himself toward the folding front doors where Ray was waiting for him.

"Good job. Now take a seat and relax while I drive." Ray reached out his hand to help Drew up.

"You always get... to drive," Drew complained breathlessly, as he moved toward the back of the bus.

Ray noticed Angie walking back toward the hospital doors. "Angie!" he called after her.

Sherry put her hand on his shoulder. "She isn't coming with us," she told him. "She's going to stay here and help the kids who weren't able to travel."

"That's crazy. She won't make it a week with the shit that's going on." Ray wanted to go after her, but he saw the look in his wife's eyes and realized that there was no use arguing.

"I tried, Ray, but she wasn't having it. You heard those kids crying up there. She said something about a sister she lost when she was a kid. I didn't get the whole story, but her mind was made up a long time before you boys got back with the bus." Sherry choked up. "We need to go."

J. H. Glaze

THIRTEEN

The bus was not in the best mechanical condition. Ray figured it had probably served many years in the education system before it was purchased for the church. He hoped it would serve their purpose now.

Sherry sat in the seat behind her husband. She tried her best to see out the window and watch for pods. So far, the sky was clear.

"Where are we going to go?" she asked.

"No choice but to head for the naval air station. Even if it's abandoned, they'll have shelters that are stocked for emergencies."

Ray slowed the bus to move past a car that had flipped over in the middle of the road.

"How're we set for gas?" Rick called out from the seat he was sharing with a little girl who was not in good shape. She had been having difficulty sitting up, and he had taken it on himself to help.

"I'll check it," Sherry offered. Standing, she could see the gas gauge. It gave her little confidence. "Shit, Ray, we only have a quarter tank. How much do you think that is in a vehicle this size?"

"I don't know how many gallons the tank holds, but I think we'll have more than enough to get where we're going." Ray continued looking straight ahead. "I'd say we're about five miles or so from our destination."

Suddenly, from the back of the bus, one of the children shouted, "They're coming! They're coming!"

The commotion woke Drew, who had just drifted off. He jumped from his seat to see what was coming. Just as he spotted the pods headed their way, the heavens opened up and it began to rain.

"Damn, I can't see very far. It's raining so hard that it's making it difficult to see out for more than twenty yards." Drew moved to the other side just as lightning crackled overhead and a loud roar of thunder rattled the windows of the old bus. "Wait, I can see a whole fleet of them coming our way. Ray, you better get this piece of shit moving!"

Ray was doing all he could to accelerate. With the rain pelting the windshield, and the worn wipers smearing his view, he was afraid he could slam into something and never see it coming.

"Everybody get away from the windows!" he yelled as loud as he could, his voice nearly drowned out by the thunder from another lightning strike. "Try not to touch the metal frame, just in case."

"In case of what?" Sherry asked, as she moved toward the aisle.

"I don't know about these buses. I think you're safe from the lightning as long as you... Damn!"

The bus jumped as he ran over a motorcycle. A handle bar caught the wheel well, and it was dragged along making a terrible sound. When they hit a pothole, it flipped off to the side of the road.

Rick helped the little girl next to him get away from the window. He had just finished tucking a blanket around her when he looked outside. "Ray, those things are almost on us. Step on it!"

Drew could see the motion from the other side of the bus and moved across the aisle. Dropping open the window, he began firing on the pods. Rick was shooting from the window on his side, but the screams from the kids were making him nervous.

"Get down on the floor!" he yelled to the kids. His hand was shaking and at least a third of the bullets missed their mark.

The pods on both sides of the bus were closing in on them. Their metallic tentacles crashed through the windows and writhed as they tried to grab the people inside. The screaming intensified and everyone dove for cover under the seats.

Ray knew that their guns would be ineffective against so many of the pods, and just as he feared, the battle was being lost. To make matters worse, the pods began to lift the bus into the air.

"Fuck!" Ray yelled as the engine revved.

The tires were off the ground now and spinning freely. He took his foot from the gas, released the wheel, and leaned down to hold Sherry for what might be their last moments alive. Sensing her panic, his heart began to race. He felt overwhelmed and helpless because he knew he couldn't save her or anyone else.

He looked to the back of the bus, and everyone but Drew was splayed on the floor. Max and the other children were crying and covering their heads. There was nothing he could do to make the horror disappear. Desperate to offer comfort, he shouted to them what he always said when things seemed hopeless.

"Don't worry, everything will be okay."

He knew he was lying.

FOURTEEN

A flash of lightning came out of nowhere and fingers of blue light enveloped the bus. It was over in an instant. The bus began shaking, jerking as they dropped onto the top of an abandoned SUV. The noise of metal scraping metal was deafening, and the kids were still screaming as the assault came to an end.

"What the hell just happened?" Ray yelled back to Drew who was lifting himself from the floor.

"Look at that shit! The lightning kicked their asses."

Drew pointed out the window at the pods, which were now lying motionless on the ground. They looked as if they had swelled and ruptured from the inside. Splits and slits riddled the surface of the main sections, and the tentacles drooped at their sides. Steam, or possibly smoke, rose up in plumes as the rain pounded everything in sight.

The children were now on their feet and looking out the windows. They pointed and whispered as though afraid that they could be overheard by the alien craft. Sherry was holding her son while Rick and Ray checked the other children for injuries as best they could. It was difficult to see in the dark of the storm.

"What do you think happened?"

Rick popped the clip out of his weapon and checked to see how many rounds remained, while Drew stuck his head out the window to survey the damage to the bus.

"I think the lightning got them." Grinning, he added, "I saw what's written on the side of the bus just now. It says 'Jesus Saves'. I think He just saved our ass with a lightning strike."

"Rick, give me a hand. We need to see the extent of the damage." Ray left Sherry to finish checking the kids and opened the door of the bus to step out.

By the time Rick reached the door, Ray was walking the length of the bus. The look on his brother's face spoke volumes. More than distress from the cold rain, it was apparent just how much trouble they were in.

The rain streamed down Ray's forehead as he bent to look under the bus. The vehicle below it was mostly crushed. The front wheels of the bus were hanging above the pavement by a few feet, but the back wheels were nearly touching the ground. Ray thought they might be able to get the bus off of the truck until he saw the driveshaft.

"Look at this shit, Rick."

His brother looked under the bus to see what Ray was talking about. "Is it broken, or just bent?"

"I think it's bent, but if it is, it may as well be broken. I don't think we'll get too far with it like that. We'd need a shop full of tools to fix it."

Rick didn't answer. Instead, he was staring at something off in the distance.

"Ray." He whispered at first, and then he raised his voice. "Ray, look!"

As Ray's gaze followed his brother's, his blood froze.

"Oh shit! Was that there before?"

"I don't know. It's been hovering there for a minute or two, but it doesn't seem to be getting any closer."

"I think we'd better get back on the bus. I have a bad feeling about this."

As soon as the words left his lips, the pods on the ground vaporized in flash of light. Ray quickly made his way toward the doors of the bus and jumped the step with Rick close behind. As soon as they were clear, Sherry was ready with the door handle and slammed it shut behind them.

Drew called from the rear of the bus, "Did you guys see that? Isn't it weird how they self-destruct after they become damaged? There are still a couple of those things hovering out there. It's like they're afraid to come any closer. I bet those fuckers think we used the lightning against the other pods."

Another bolt of lightning shot from the sky and struck one of the pods that had been keeping its distance, causing it to split right up the middle. It spilled its contents to the pavement before crash landing several feet away.

Everyone gasped as something crawled from the pile of slop on the pavement. An appendage resembling an arm reached up to the sky followed by another one just like it. As the rain continued to fall, a bulbous head lifted a few inches off the ground. Except for the malformed limbs, the alien creature was nothing more than a blob of thick goo.

"Hostage!"

Drew was shouting as he ran from the back of the bus and threw open the doors before anyone could stop him. They watched in shock as he struggled to lift the slimy creature from the pile of equipment surrounding it. After several attempts, he grabbed it by the arms. It stretched a bit as he pulled it toward the bus, and its many legs dragged behind as he made his way to the door.

"Thing is heavier than it looks and smells like ass."

He heaved as he lifted his hostage up the step and dropped it in the aisle. The kids screamed as it squirmed on the floor. The alien appeared to have no spine as it reached for the edge of one of the seats and tried to pull itself up. Something akin to eyes moved just under the skin, and it gasped for breath through the slits in its sides.

Drew wiped his hands on his pants. "Damn things are slimy. Ugly as shit, too, don't ya think?"

Ray was holding a gun pointed at their prisoner. "What the hell are we gonna do with this?"

Sherry didn't hesitate. "Human shield... er, alien shield. If they try to come closer, we'll threaten to kill this one."

Rick and Ray just stared at her as Drew nodded enthusiastically. "Exactly what I had in mind."

The children were watching in silence, except for Mike. He was digging in his pocket for the knife his father had given him for his birthday last year. When he got his hand on it, he pulled it out and opened it. Stepping forward, he poked the alien near the end of one of its snaky legs. It shrieked as it pulled the leg into its body.

"That's how we threaten it." The teen firmly gripped the knife. "If those pods come close, we jab it again. I bet they will hear it scream."

Indeed, the pods that had been hovering close by moved a bit further away.

"Hey, he's right," Rick confirmed.

"Okay, then, here's our choice. We can stay here and hope for some help to come along, or we can make a run for it." Ray scanned their faces and shared their sense of futility. "Yeah, I know it doesn't sound good either way."

"Whatever we do, we need to be quick about it," Drew answered. "We don't know how long this fuckin' monster will live outside of its ship." He kicked the alien and it shrieked again. "Piece of shit motherfucker!"

"Language," Sherry inserted, nodding toward the kids.

"Alright, everybody, get ready to move." Ray began gathering the kids near the front of the bus. He started moving them toward the door.

The hiss of something flying past the bus took everyone by surprise, and the projectile hit its mark with a loud explosion. Rick's eyes followed the smoke trail back to its origin and saw the camouflage clad men advancing on them. "Holy shit, soldiers!"

He pointed out the front window, and when Ray turned to look, he saw about fifty soldiers and heavily armored vehicles moving toward them.

FIFTEEN

The officer in command of the unit stood in the aisle of the bus staring down at the alien hostage. Taking off his headgear, he wiped the sweat from his brow.

"Ugly sons-a-bitches. How'd you catch this one?"

Ray was looking out at the crash site. "It got tossed when a bolt of lightning struck its pod. Damn thing cracked like an egg and dumped him on the road."

"The other ones don't like when you hurt it," Max added. "It screams when you poke it."

"You don't say. Well, I guess we just learned something that might help us get back to the base."

He yelled out the door, "Load these kids and their supplies on the transport, then put this thing in the storage compartment. Get it tied down somehow. I need two armed men guarding it."

Turning his attention back to Max, he added, "Let's get you folks back to the base. We can get some medical help for you kids and have somebody check this ugly bastard out."

"The base is still intact?" Ray asked.

"When we left, it sure was. We knew early on this morning something wasn't right, so we got prepared for whatever was coming. When they hit, we kicked their ass in the first few minutes. I don't think they are used to taking casualties, 'cause they haven't tried to move on the base since first assault."

"That explains why they hung back after the lightning struck," Drew said.

Sherry interrupted, "I was afraid we were going to have to walk somewhere carrying these kids."

"I was going to ask, where the hell did you get all these kids?" The commander watched as his men helped them out of the bus through the back door.

"We took shelter in a hospital. They'd been left behind."

"They were lucky you found them, even more so that you brought them with you. Now let's get them to some shelter. Captain!"

"Yes, sir."

"Get these folks back to the base, take whatever equipment you need and call in some replacements. Move it, soldier."

"Yes, sir."

Ray shook the commander's hand and thanked him for his help. He turned and walked with his family to the truck, which was waiting to take them to a place where they could ride out the remainder of the assault they had miraculously survived.

.

SIXTEEN

The convoy of three specialized vehicles snaked through the stalled traffic as they made their way to the naval base. The lead vehicle, an armored troop transport with a reinforced front bumper, carried most of the children from the hospital.

Drew and Rick rode in the second vehicle with a few of the kids who were able to walk. Behind them, Ray rode with Sherry and Max along with the remainder of the soldiers. The rain had all but stopped, and the ride was rough. Occasionally, the lead vehicle had to push a disabled car to make room for the others to pass.

Sherry was watching through a small window. "The exit for the base is one mile," she read from a roadside sign.

"I hope we make it," Max whispered.

"Don't worry, sweetie. We are safe now with these soldiers. They have everything they need to…"

WHAM!

Sherry was cut short when something ran out from between two tall buildings. It slammed into the first transport vehicle, knocking it over on its side. With the sound of screeching metal piercing the air, it slid to a stop.

Ray was trying to see through the front windows of their vehicle, but they were too smeared to get a good look. "Do not get out of that seat no matter what happens," he cautioned his family before unfastening his seatbelt.

The door on the back of the vehicle opened and three soldiers stepped out into the street carrying some large weapons Ray had never seen before. He spotted some rifles on a special rack by the door. Grabbing a gun and a shoulder bag of ammunition, he slipped down to the ground behind the soldiers.

Once he got around the back of the vehicle, he saw the horror that had brought them to a halt. The transport bus was on its side and a large Mech was viciously tearing at the bottom of its frame with sharp claws. He could hear the shrill screams of the terrorized children as the under carriage was being assaulted.

The soldiers inched forward with their weapons aimed, but no one fired. At the same time, the back door of the second vehicle opened and armed soldiers came rushing out with Drew and Rick close behind holding weapons at the ready.

"What the fuck! Someone take that thing out!" Ray shouted.

One of the soldiers turned and answered him. "These weapons are too powerful at this range. They'll kill everybody in there if we fire."

Drew looked at Ray, then turned to Rick and said, "Get my back, bro. Take that fucker out when I draw it away."

Before Rick could respond, Drew ran toward the Mech screaming, "Hey, you motherfucker! Over here! Come get my ass."

He fired his pistol at the thing as he yelled, running past it as fast as his legs would carry him. He was surprised that he had made enough noise to take its attention away from the transport. It let go of the wheel it was crushing in its claw and turned to pursue him.

Drew could run fast for someone his size, but when the Mech began to move, it was right at his heels. At about twenty-five yards out, he screamed, "Shoot it! Shoot the motherfucker!"

The soldiers hesitated. The man would be killed by the blast if they fired. Drew seemed to understand their predicament. He came to a sudden stop, then turned and took aim at the Mech. He screamed and fired on it even as it slid to a halt in front of him. With tremendous force, it brought one of its great arms down and dealt a crushing blow. Drew disappeared beneath it in a cloud of red spray just as the command was given to fire.

Projectiles screeched through the air striking the mechanical beast. The explosions created a shockwave that blew everyone not taking cover to the ground. When Ray was pulled to his feet by one of the soldiers, he saw the pile of twisted metal that remained. He knew that Drew was under there somewhere, and his eyes clouded over with tears. Scanning the scene to see what had become of Rick, he saw his brother lying on the ground.

"Rick!" he yelled as he ran to him. Finding him unconscious, he looked around for help, but the soldiers were busy helping children from the disabled vehicle and loading them into the remaining transports. He checked Rick for a pulse and was relieved to find him alive. Tossing his brother over his shoulder, he carried him to where Sherry and Max were waiting for him.

"Please, do whatever you can to help him. I need to get back to the others."

Sherry dragged Rick into the vehicle while Ray ran to the bus and helped carry the children. When the last one was pulled out, the soldier who had been working inside the bus reported that at least a dozen of them had not survived.

Ray's guilt caught up with him. Perhaps they might have been better off if he had not taken them from the hospital. It was too late for him to doubt himself. He ran back to check on his family, but when he got there, he found soldiers standing around the transport with the door closing.

"Hey, my family is in there." He tried to look in as the door clacked shut.

"It's a full house, buddy. We're gonna have to ride on the outside." The soldier stepped up and offered Ray a hand. "Put your feet on that ledge and use the handholds. It's a tougher ride, but we'll have better eyes on the enemy."

Ray stepped up on the side of the vehicle and saw that the one ahead was covered with soldiers as well. An order was given and the two transports began moving around the wrecked bus and onward to their destination once again.

J. H. Glaze

.

SEVENTEEN

As they turned the corner behind the lead vehicle, Ray could see the gate of the military compound. This was where he had been headed since he and his family had escaped the destruction of their home. It was hard to believe they had made it here alive. With the sun low in the sky, he was relieved that this day was finally coming to a close.

After they were waved through the gate, the soldiers began jumping off the transports and walking toward a concrete structure that appeared to be the entrance to an underground bunker. Ray stayed where he was and rode to the staging area next to the entrance. There was a lot of activity in this crowded space. The troops were gearing up for another mission while survivors were being triaged according to their needs.

When the vehicle rolled to a stop, Ray jumped down and went to the back to wait for his family. The kids had already begun filing out, all sweaty and red-faced. The heat of all of those bodies packed inside the tight quarters must have been near overwhelming. Finally, he saw Sherry and Max coming out with Rick right behind them. He was conscious and alert, though not at all cheerful.

"Hey, bro," he called to Ray. "I tried to get them to let me out to ride shotgun with you, but there was no way they were going to stop. Like a guy who almost gets his ass blown off can't be useful!"

Ray hugged his brother and took him by the shoulders. "No problem, just good to have you alive and talking shit again."

Sherry and Max were standing at a distance watching the reunion when gunfire erupted and someone yelled, "Incoming!"

A fleet of pods had flown in from their blind side, snatching up both soldiers and civilians. While breaking skyward, loaded with more than they could carry, the ground was peppered with captives that slipped from their grip. Some of the pods were destroyed as the soldiers fought back. The automatic weapon fire and grenade explosions sent them slamming back to earth.

Ray was surrounded by chaos and spun around when he heard a familiar scream from behind. He watched in horror as his wife and son were swept up by the tentacles of one of the pods. Sherry desperately reached for Max as they were taken up toward the clouds and out of sight.

"Sherry! Max!" Ray cried out as he started running after them.

Rick grabbed his brother and tried to pull him back.

"They're gone, Ray. We'll get them back. We'll find a way." He tried dragging his brother toward the entrance to the compound, but he was still weak and didn't get far.

"Motherfuckers! No! I'm coming for you, Max. I'm coming," Ray shouted to the sky.

He stopped struggling, realizing that he would need some serious help before he could retrieve his family. The horror fell upon him like a ton of bricks. He was so overwhelmed he nearly collapsed, but he gathered every bit of strength he could muster and turned to Rick. "We need to go."

***

"I need the person in charge. Now!" Rick barked at a soldier who was placing bands around the arms of survivors and scanning them.

Another soldier asked, "What seems to be the problem, sir?"

Ray stepped in. "My wife and son were just taken by one of those fuckers. I need something with some firepower to stop them. Where can I get some weapons?"

"I'm terribly sorry, sir. If they have been taken, then they are probably…"

"No! Don't fuckin' tell me that. I need some big guns or a bomb or something. I'm going after them." Ray saw the confusion in the soldier's face and added, "C4, do you have any explosives here?"

"I… I think so. You need to talk to the CO. He has to authorize any…"

"Right, so take me to him now! I don't have time to fuck around."

Ray looked around the room for an officer or someone more able to help. Seeing his determination, the soldier turned on his heels.

"Follow me, sir."

EIGHTEEN

In the office, Ray paced impatiently as he waited. He sat in the chair and put his head down, cradling it in his hands as tears began to flow. When the officer finally came in, he wiped his eyes and stood to meet him.

"My men said you want to see me? I don't have much time, so make it brief."

"Yes, I can make it very brief. My wife and son were taken by one of the pods right outside this building just after we arrived. I'm going after them. I need explosives, C4 and detonators if you have them."

"Sir, we have the explosives, but there is no way we can get you to that ship. We don't have..."

"Look, I'm not asking you to take me. Just get me the shit I need and I'll get a ride."

"How, may I ask?"

"From those fuckin' pods! Has anybody been sent yet to stop those bastards? I'm volunteering right now."

The officer was stunned. "If you think you can do that, you're either crazy or the bravest son of a bitch I've ever met."

"Please, just get me the explosives. I'm going after my wife and son, and I want to wreak some havoc on those fucks while I'm at it."

"Do you even know how to use that stuff? I don't want you to blow yourself up."

"Look, I was in the Marines and did two tours before I was discharged. We took out concrete bunkers in the Gulf with that shit. Do I have to show you what I can..."

"No, man, just give me a minute."

The officer picked up his phone. Pushing a few buttons, he paused and looked at Ray before addressing the person on the line. "Washington, bring two satchels of C4 with detonators to my office ASAP. No questions, soldier, do it now."

He hung up the phone and looked at Ray. "I don't know who is crazier, you for asking for this or me for going along with it. I just hope this ends well for all concerned."

"Me too, sir, me too."

"So what's your plan, Mr. Badass?"

"The name's Ray. I'm going to get to the ship and find my wife and my son. I'll set the charges and get us the hell out."

"Soooo... what about the rest of the people up there? Any plans to rescue them?"

"How would I do that?" Ray sounded irritated.

"Honestly, I don't know how you do any of it. The whole thing sounds like a suicide mission if you ask me. You'll likely get yourself and your family killed."

"Look, if I don't do this they are dead anyway. Right? So there is no other option."

Ray looked over the officer's shoulder at the security monitor mounted on the wall. There were four divided screens, and one of them had a view of some planes in a hangar. "Do you do any jump training here?"

"You a pilot, too?" The officer looked toward the monitor.

"No, but I'm guessing you have parachutes if you do."

"Sure we do."

"Good, I need three of those chutes."

The officer tried not to smile. "Let me get this straight. You are planning to get yourself grabbed by one of those pod fuckers while you are packing a couple satchels of C4 and three parachutes?"

"What about it?"

"Aliens might wonder if you're planning on moving in with all that baggage."

He paused, looked around, and then suggested, "Look, we can put all that shit in one of our assault packs. Do you think you'll be able to get into the ship with it?"

"I doubt they're gonna scan my bags at some checkpoint. Load it up. I need a detonator though. If they try to take the bag, I'll end it right there."

Just at that moment, the soldier who had been ordered to bring the explosives burst into the room carrying two satchels. "Here you go, sir. I brought you some remote detonators, just in case. You're good to go."

"Thanks, Washington. Please escort Ray here to the hangar and get him an assault pack and some parachutes. Be sure to check your six out there."

NINETEEN

When Ray stepped out of the office, he could hear Rick arguing with another soldier nearby.

"Look, I need to get in there. My brother's in there. He's going to need help with whatever he has planned for those alien assholes."

Ray yelled across the busy room. "Rick! Bro, come on."

He followed the soldier toward the exit while his brother navigated through all the people coming and going. When they got outside, he handed Rick the two satchels.

"Hold on to these, I'm getting some parachutes."

"Parachutes? For what?"

"I'm going up there to get Sherry and Max, blow the aliens to hell, and maybe turn the tide on this shit storm."

"Well, I'm going too, then. Get an extra chute."

"I can't let you go, man. This is probably a one-way ticket. I don't even know if I will be able to find them. You saw how big that ship is."

Rick grabbed hold of his brother's arm. "Ray, all of our lives we've had each others backs. It's not going to stop here, not now. I'm going with you."

"Right."

Rick stood strong and determined, and there was no time for arguing. Ray turned to the soldier who had been waiting for him. "I need an extra parachute, four instead of three, and we need to get them quick," he instructed.

The soldier nodded and led them through the crowd. He scanned a card at the door to the hangar. When the lock clicked open, they stepped into the spacious building. Passing several large planes stored out on the shiny concrete floor, the soldier led them to a fenced area in the back. Inside, he opened a cabinet and began pulling parachutes from it. "Four?"

Ray nodded. "And I'll need an assault pack to carry them."

"Make it two packs," Rick said. To Ray, he explained, "I need to take one of those bombs and my own chute in case we get separated up there."

"Good plan."

A few minutes later, the packs were loaded with their lethal cargo. The brothers took turns helping each other strap them on, making certain they were as secure as possible. When the last strap was buckled, Ray turned to his brother. "Ready, bro?"

TWENTY

Outside the hangar, the brothers walked toward an open field across the concrete tarmac. Ray's gaze was turned skyward.

"Stay close. I want us to ride the same taxi on the way up."

Rick moved closer and was about to respond when he heard a whoosh behind them. Before he could turn around, two tentacles stretched down from the pod and grabbed them. In an instant, they were rocketing toward the clouds.

Ray could see the pained look on his brother's face, and he was certain it mirrored his own. The tentacles that held them were not only squeezing the life out of them, but the sting they administered was like an electric shock and felt like burning fire.

"Hang on, Rick!" he yelled. He wasn't sure if his brother could hear him.

Finally, he replied, "It fucking hurts like hell!"

Within moments, they were approaching the massive ship they had only been able to glimpse before. At this altitude, they were above the clouds and the sun was still visible, clear and bright. It dawned on Ray that he should be having trouble breathing from the lack of oxygen, but he was having no trouble at all.

"Can you breathe okay?" he yelled at Rick, and his brother nodded.

"Here we go!" He pointed toward an opening that had appeared on the smooth side of the ship. Almost organic in nature, it rippled back to create an opening large enough for the full load of a pod and its captives.

Holding its cargo tightly in its grip, the pod shifted and slid through the opening. It traveled a short way through a narrow tunnel lit with bright blue light before passing into a small room and dropping the brothers on a soft surface. As their eyes adjusted to the dim light, they realized the pod had disappeared and they were alone.

"You alright, Ray?"

"Yeah, you?"

"Pretty sore from that fucker, but yeah."

Rick was cut short by a hissing sound as a heavy green mist fell from above and they began coughing from the horrid smell. When the mist cleared, a flash of white light left them blinded and completely dry. No sooner did their eyes adjust from the flash, than the floor stretched down into a funnel shape.

They both tumbled at the expanding edge and slid down through a tube that dropped them into a cavernous chamber. As they hit the floor, Ray saw the tube retract into the ceiling from where it had come.

"What the fuck?" Ray looked around the massive room. It was hundreds of feet high and appeared to be many times longer. The walls were a honeycomb of individual cells.

"Ray, come on. I see something," Rick called as he ran toward one of the walls. As they approached it, they could see that each contained at least one human captive.

"Holy shit!" Horrified, Rick looked down the length of the wall. "I can't even imagine how many people are in here. If we blow this thing up, they're all dead."

"Dammit. Motherfuckers!" Ray felt sick to his stomach. He might never find his family in this enormous ship.

As the brothers stood there feeling overwhelmed, something latched onto them from behind. Before they knew what had happened, they both went limp, but remained fully conscious. Whatever had grabbed them was now carrying them down the main walkway through the ship.

Ray couldn't feel his arms or legs. His body was as useless as a shirt hanging on a clothesline. Somehow, he managed to push out a few words. "Bastards! Where are you taking us?" As he swung in it's grip, he nearly pissed himself when he realized his captor was similar to the Mech that had crushed Drew in the battle outside the base.

The machine stopped in front of the wall of cells. A ring of light encircled them as the floor beneath their feet began to rise like an elevator. They shot into the air, still in the clutches of the machine.

When they finally came to a stop, the brothers were hundreds of feet above the floor and directly in front of one of the honeycomb cells. The door was translucent, and they could see that there was someone inside. When the door slid back, they heard the voice of a boy say, "Dad?"

Ray's heart was pounding. "Max?

The machine moved forward and set them on the floor of the chamber. When it stepped back, the door slid shut behind it.

"Ray? Rick? Oh my God!" Sherry stood up and moved from the back of the small space and fell to her knees to embrace her husband. "I didn't know if you were alive or..."

"We came as fast as we could." He pulled himself to his knees. "What's happening here?"

"I don't know, honey. They brought us here and left us. They gave us something that looked like food and water through an opening in the wall, but we are afraid to eat any of it."

"Food and water? This doesn't make any sense." Rick had stood up and was trying to look outside the cell.

"What the fuck is going on?" He repeated his question, yelling through the door, "What the fuck is going on?"

Sherry helped Ray release himself from the heavy pack that was still strapped to his back. "What is this?"

"Parachutes and... We thought we could find you, set some charges, and bail before they were about to detonate. These satchels are explosive, enough to take out a whole city block. We might have been able to stop these bastards, but now I don't see how we can do it without killing everyone up here."

There was silence as they looked at each other in despair.

"But, Dad, they might capture everyone down there if we don't stop them. Right?"

J. H. Glaze

"I'm sorry, Max. You might be right. Unfortunately, I don't think we can stop them this way. Too many would die if we did."

"We're all gonna die anyway, Dad. I think those things want to eat us. I don't want to get eaten." He started to cry, but stopped and wiped the tears from his eyes. "We should blow them all up, Dad. We can save all the other people down there on the ground."

Ray hugged his brave son. He was so proud of Max in that moment for demonstrating such courage and willingness to sacrifice himself for others. That level of humanity was well beyond his years. The lump in his throat prevented him from saying a word.

Rick filled the gap. "You understand what you are saying, right, bud?"

"I do, Uncle Rick. We might not get to live, but everyone down there will. And, I don't want to get eaten. I've seen the movies. I know what they do."

He turned to his dad. "Blow em up, Dad. We'll be like heroes! Maybe even be on TV. How we saved everybody."

Ray looked at Sherry who was nodding her agreement. "Max is right. We have no choice. It's the only chance they have down there."

"Rick, help me out here." Ray looked to his brother for a final answer.

"I think they're right, man. We might give them a chance to make it."

Ray looked toward the door, "Fuck." He picked up the pack and pulled the remote detonator from a pocket on the side of it.

"Gimme yours, Rick. If we set them off at the same time, we might at least blow a hole in this thing and bring it all down. It will happen so fast, we won't feel a thing."

"Come on. Let's have a hug before we do this." Ray stood up and reached out to the others.

Sherry was smiling, but tears streamed down her cheeks. "Let's say our goodbyes. We can share what we think was best about the world we're leaving behind. Ray, you go last, and when you're done, push that button before I chicken out, okay?" She hugged her family as hard as she could. "Don't give us a warning, honey, just do it."

Ray didn't say a word.

"I'll go first," Rick volunteered. "You must know how much I love you guys. In fact, if Ray hadn't asked you out, Sherry, I would have."

Ray glared at his brother, and then smiled and nodded.

"I've had the best life a guy like me could ask for. I got to spend a good part of it living and hiking in some of the most beautiful mountain ranges. I want others to have the chance to experience it." He nodded as he finished.

Max spoke next. "Mom and Dad, you guys are the best, so much better than any of my friends' parents. I love you both very very much."

The tears began to roll down Ray's cheeks. Sherry covered her face to hide the pain she felt. Ray squeezed her hand as Max continued. "I'm leaving behind the beaches, so the kids who are left can keep building the best sandcastles. Go ahead, Mom."

Sherry choked at first, and then began, "I love you all so much. I know we will be together forever after this." She took a deep breath and began again. "To all those on earth, I leave the chance to have a beautiful life with a loving family and a safe place to call home. A place where they can be together and give each other love and comfort." She paused before saying, "Go ahead, honey."

Ray looked at each one of them as he spoke. "I planned for the worst in the event that this day might come, so we could survive it. I'm sorry things didn't go as I planned." He placed his thumb over the button on the detonator. "I leave behind the hope that mankind might learn something from all this, and…"

His speech was cut short by the sound of a booming foghorn. It shook the walls of the cell, and they held on tightly to each other's hands. At the same time, the door to their cell became as transparent as glass. Lights began to pulsate, and a giant hologram of Earth hovered above the floor just outside their door.

The image turned slowly before them. It seemed to shake and bright orange flashes appeared near the west coast of the USA, at the horn of Africa, in the heart of Europe, and flames shot out from them. Giant cracks spread out from those places, covering the surface of Earth as far as they could see.

In a moment, the entire planet shuddered and came apart in a violent explosion. Seconds later, a massive boom rocked the chamber and shook as though an earthquake was taking the ship down.

"Did that actually happen?" Rick stared at the image as the last bits of the planet dissolved into darkness.

Ray took his thumb off the detonator button. "What the hell?"

"It felt like the earth really exploded," said Sherry, as the scene faded. "That was a shockwave, wasn't it?"

Ray was stunned. "I can't believe it. Have we just been rescued by aliens? Did these bastards bring us here to save us?"

TWENTY ONE

Something pulled at the cloth of Ray's pant leg. At first, he ignored it. He was still thinking about the light show, and the possibility that they had survived a cataclysmic event. The feeling of relief washed around his brain like a warm ocean breeze. Then a distant sound, a familiar sound, broke the trance and he was back to reality.

He looked down to see what had caused the tugging sensation. Through glazed eyes, he realized it was Max. The boy was lying close to him on the floor of the cell, his hand grasping the cloth of his pant leg.

Max He shrieked as he sunk further down, and a look of fear and agony spread across his face. "Dad! Dad, push the button!" He went silent, as he was absorbed into the floor.

Behind him, Rick and Sherry were trying to help each other, but they were quickly sinking. Realizing he could no longer feel his own feet, Ray looked down to see that he was already up to his knees in thick goo where only moments before had been a solid floor beneath him.

It was then he felt the pain. Quickly, his mind flashed through the series of events that had led to this moment. Were the cells in the great hall actually fuel cells? Were the captives inside them converted to fuel to power the massive ship? It almost made sense to him as he continued to be drawn down into the floor.

He looked at the hand that had held the remote control for the detonators.   shot through him when he realized it was no longer in his grasp. He was confused, and he tried to move his arm, which hung useless at his side.

His eyes searched below him for the remote, and he finally spotted it partially sunken into the floor. Like a rag doll in a dance contest, he jerked and shivered as he tried to reach for it. He pulled at his legs with every ounce of his fading strength until finally he broke free. Just below his knees, his legs were gone, dissolved and dripping like melted candles, and he toppled to the floor.

Ray lay helpless upon the remains of his son. He could see the remote detonator only inches from his hand and strained to reach it, but he could not. He was dying, just like Max.

All was quiet around him. His family had ceased any sound or movement. He was sinking, half dissolved into the floor, when suddenly his body convulsed. With super human effort, he opened his mouth and screamed his son's name. "Max!"

His fingers reached the button of the detonator and twitched just enough to push it.

The explosion set off a chain reaction within the fuel cells. In a few violent seconds, the entire ship erupted, exploding into a shower of metal shards and organic slop that rained down to the ground below.

***

The soldiers at the base stared at the sky as the thumping sound and flash above gave testament that the father who had risked everything for his family had accomplished his mission. Yet, as they watched the flaming remnants of the ship falling in the dark sky, not a single parachute was visible.

With awe and respect, they stopped what they were doing, stood at attention and saluted. Returning to their tasks, they worked to ensure that the survivors of this fateful day would be safe through the night, not knowing what the new morning might bring.

J. H. Glaze